Growing Readers

Purchased with New Hanover County
Partnership for Children Funds

Grandpa Bear's Christmas

Bonnie Pryor

Illustrated by Bruce Degen

William Morrow & Co., New York

Text copyright © 1986 by Bonnie Pryor
Illustrations copyright © 1986 by Bruce Degen
All rights reserved. No part of this book may be reproduced or utilized in any form or by any means, electronic or
mechanical, including photocopying, recording or by any information storage and retrieval system, without permission in
writing from the Publisher. Inquiries should be addressed to William Morrow and Company, Inc., 105 Madison Avenue,
New York, NY 10016. Printed in Hong Kong
1 2 3 4 5 6 7 8 9 10
Library of Congress Cataloging-in-Publication Data
Pryor, Bonnie.
Grandpa Bear's Christmas.
Summary: The Bear family's winter adventures prepare them for Christmas.
[1. Bears—Fiction. 2. Christmas—Fiction]
I. Degen, Bruce, ill. II. Title.
PZ7.P94965Gt 1986   [E]   85-29707
ISBN 0-688-06063-3
ISBN 0-688-06064-1 (lib. bdg.)

for Matthew, the newest—B.P.

for Grandpa and Grandma, Bill and Revella—B.D.

One

"Winter is my favorite time of year," said Grandpa Bear. "Outside it is very cold. But inside I can sit by the fire and be as snug as a bug in a rug."

Harry Bear looked out the window at the snow. "Winter is the time for riding sleds and making snowmen—not for taking naps by the fire," he said.

"Let's make a snowman," said Samantha. "I can help you."

"I am going to make a big snowman," said Harry Bear. "It will be bigger than our house. It will be as tall as the trees. You are too little. I will make it all by myself."

Harry Bear put on his coat and went outside to make a snowman.

Samantha Bear looked out the window. "I want to go outside and make a snowman, too," she said.

"I have to give Baby Bear his bath now," said Mama Bear. "Maybe later I can help you. Why don't you play with your trucks or make a city out of blocks?"

Samantha made a tower with her blocks. But just as she put on the last block, the tower fell down, and some of the blocks rolled under the chair.

"I'm tired of playing with these dumb old blocks," Samantha said crossly. "I wish I could make a snowman like Harry Bear."

Grandpa Bear opened his eyes. "Once I made the biggest snowman in the world," he said. He shut his eyes again. "That was how I met my old friend Santa Claus."

"Did you really meet Santa Claus?" asked Samantha.

"Oh, yes," said Grandpa Bear. "Of course that was long ago. Santa was much younger then."

"Tell me about it," said Samantha Bear. She sat on Grandpa's lap.

"Well," said Grandpa Bear. "I think it must have started when I decided to make a snowman. I wanted to make it very big, but I was too small. Then I had an idea. I would make the snowman on top of a hill. That would make him look much taller."

"Did it work?" Samantha asked.

"Yes, indeed," said Grandpa Bear. "He was a very nice snowman. I gave him a scarf and a hat, and even some buttons for his coat. Then I remembered an old broom I had found on Halloween night. 'That will make the snowman look even better,' I said to myself. So I went back to the house and got the old broom out of the closet."

"But Grandpa, how did you meet Santa Claus?" asked
Samantha.

"Wait," said Grandpa Bear. "I am coming to that part.
As soon as I gave that broom to the snowman, he began to
talk. And, oh, was he ever grouchy.

" 'Well,' said the snowman. 'You certainly did not make
me very big! Is this the best you could do?'

" 'I am very sorry,' I said. 'As you see, I am only a very
small bear. But I did put you up on this hill so you would
look bigger.'

" 'That's another thing,' grumbled the snowman. 'How
can anyone see how wonderful I am way up here on this
hill? Take me to town this minute.'

" 'I don't think that is a very good idea,' I said.

" 'If you won't take me, then I will go by myself,' said the snowman. He took one step. Then—oops!—he slipped. Away he went right over the top of the hill. Over and over he rolled, getting bigger and bigger. 'Help, help,' he cried. 'I order you to stop me this instant.' "

"Is that when you saw Santa Claus?" asked Samantha Bear.

"Soon," answered Grandpa Bear. "I ran after the snowman, but he was rolling too fast to catch. At last— THUMP!—he rolled right into a little house."

"Where was that?" asked Samantha.

"I am not sure," said Grandpa Bear. "There was a sign in front of the door reading TOY SHOP, and there was a barn with some deer that knew how to fly, and a sleigh nearby."

"It was the North Pole," said Samantha.

"I believe you may be right," nodded Grandpa Bear. "I was standing there wondering what to do when a nice fat man with a red suit and a long white beard came running to the toy shop."

"That must have been Santa Claus," said Samantha.

"That is exactly what he said his name was," said Grandpa Bear. "He was very unhappy because it was time to load up the toys and this snowman was blocking the door. But the snowman wouldn't move, even when we asked him very politely.

" 'Oh, no,' he said in a grouchy voice. 'I am very dizzy. How would you like to roll over and over like that? I am going to stand right here and never move.'

"It looked like none of the children were going to get their presents that year. Santa was dreadfully worried."

"What did you do?"

"I thought and I thought," said Grandpa Bear. "Then I had an idea. I made a nice fire to warm up my hands. 'You must be very cold,' I said to the snowman. 'Why don't you warm yourself by the fire?'

" 'I am a little chilly,' said the snowman. He moved just a little closer to the fire. All of a sudden, that snowman began to melt. He got smaller and smaller. Soon there was nothing left but a big puddle. Santa was very happy. He loaded up the presents and gave me a ride home in his sleigh."

Just then Harry Bear came back in the house. "It is hard work making a snowman. Would you help, Grandpa Bear?"

"We will all help," said Grandpa Bear.

They all went outside. Harry Bear rolled a great big snowball to make the bottom of the snowman. Grandpa Bear and Samantha Bear rolled a medium-sized snowball to make the middle of the snowman, and Mama Bear and Baby Bear rolled a little snowball for the head. They made eyes from pieces of coal and put a hat and scarf on him.

"It needs something else," said Harry Bear. "Maybe I'll give him that old broom in the closet."

"Oh, no," said Grandpa Bear and Samantha Bear. "This snowman is perfect, just the way he is."

When they went back in the house, Mama Bear made everyone some cocoa. Then they all sat by the fire, as snug as bugs in a rug.

TWO

"Let's go for a walk in the snow," said Grandpa Bear one day.

"Oh, yes," said Samantha Bear. She put on her warm winter coat and her boots. She put on her new mittens and her hat. Then Grandpa Bear put on his coat.

Pop! Off came a button. Pop! Off came another button. "Oh, dear," said Grandpa Bear. "I am getting too fat. Maybe I will have to go on a diet."

"Walking is good exercise," said Samantha. "Maybe after our walk your coat will fit again."

Grandpa Bear and Samantha walked in the snow. Samantha walked backward so she could see their footprints.

"Walking in snow makes me hungry," said Grandpa Bear. "Snow reminds me of ice cream."

They walked to the ice-cream shop. "What kind do you have?" asked Grandpa Bear.

"We have vanilla, chocolate, and caramel crunch."

"Oh, dear. Those are all my favorite flavors," said Grandpa Bear. "How can I choose? I will have some of each."

Samantha ate a bowl of chocolate. "I wonder if the animals at the zoo like the snow," she said when they were done.

Grandpa and Samantha walked to the zoo.

A kangaroo looked very unhappy. "Don't you like winter?" asked Samantha.

"Oh, yes," said the kangaroo. "But I was teaching my child to ice-skate, and now I can't find him anywhere."

"Perhaps he crawled into your pocket to stay warm," said Grandpa Bear.

"Why didn't I think of that?" asked the kangaroo. She reached into her pocket and pulled out her child. "Now, Henry," she said. "You know it is time for your skiing lesson." She turned to Grandpa Bear and said, "How can I ever thank you?"

"We were glad to help," said Grandpa Bear.

"I have lost something, too," said a lion.

"What did you lose?" asked Samantha.

"I have lost my dinner. Please come in and help me find it."

Samantha Bear looked at the lion. She saw his hungry smile and his big sharp teeth.

"We would love to stay and help you," said Grandpa Bear very politely. "But we must hurry home for our own dinner."

Samantha and Grandpa Bear hurried away from the zoo. "Whew," said Grandpa Bear. "Running is very hard on my old bones. I think I will sit on this bench and rest." He saw a man selling popcorn. Grandpa Bear bought a bag for himself and one for Samantha.

Samantha made angels in the snow while Grandpa Bear rested his tired bones. Then they walked home together.

"I don't understand," said Grandpa Bear. "All of this walking, and I still cannot button my coat. Perhaps I am not really fat. Perhaps my coat is just too small." Grandpa Bear smiled. "I am glad I figured that out. Now we can go home and eat our dinner. I am as hungry as a bear."

Three

"It is almost time for Christmas," said Grandpa Bear one day. "I can feel it in the air."

"I don't feel anything," said Samantha Bear.

"You don't?" asked Grandpa Bear. He looked very surprised. "Ahh," he nodded. "I know what is wrong. It is because we don't have a Christmas tree."

"I can help you chop down a tree," said Harry Bear. "Look how strong I am." He showed Grandpa Bear his muscles.

"I can see that Harry Bear is getting very strong," said Grandpa Bear. "But someone must pick out the very best tree for us to chop."

"I can do that," said Samantha. "I know just what kind of tree to pick. It will be the best one in the whole forest."

"Hooray!" said Baby Bear.

"Baby Bear must come, too," said Grandpa Bear. "We will need someone to say 'Hooray!' when we are done."

Grandpa Bear put on his coat. "Oh, dear," he said. "My coat is getting smaller and smaller. What shall I do?"

"Why don't you tell your old friend Santa?" asked Samantha. "Maybe he would bring you a big new coat."

"Santa is very busy remembering all the children," said Grandpa. "He is too busy for an old Grandpa Bear."

They walked through the snow to the woods. Samantha looked for the perfect tree. Grandpa Bear, Harry Bear, and Baby Bear sat on a rock and waited.

"Hurry," said Harry Bear. "My toes are getting cold."

Samantha looked and looked. None of the trees were just right.

"How about this one?" said Harry Bear.

"Too skinny," said Samantha Bear.

"This one is nice," said Grandpa Bear.

"Too fat," said Samantha Bear.

"Hurry," said Harry Bear. "Now my nose is getting cold."

At last Samantha found the perfect tree. It was not too tall. It was not too short. It was not too skinny or too fat. It was just the right size.

Grandpa Bear walked all around the tree. "This is the best tree in the whole woods. Samantha is very good at picking out trees."

"Hooray!" said Baby Bear.

"Let's hurry and take it home," said Harry Bear. "Now my ears are getting cold."

Grandpa Bear and Harry Bear chopped down the tree. They put it on a sled to carry home.

Baby Bear clapped his hands. "Hooray!" he said again.

Grandpa Bear, Harry Bear, and Samantha all pulled the sled back home. Baby Bear rode on top because he was too little. They brought the tree into the house and stood it in the corner.

"Wonderful," said Mama Bear.

Harry Bear and Samantha made paper chains to put on the tree, and Mama Bear and Grandpa Bear made strings of popcorn.

"Something is missing," said Samantha Bear. "We forgot to put on the star." Grandpa Bear held Samantha way up high so she could put the star on.

"Now," said Grandpa Bear. "Close your eyes and see if you can feel Christmas in the air."

Samantha Bear closed her eyes. She could smell the tree and hear the quiet of the snow. Far away someone was ringing a little bell. It felt just like Christmas.

"I can feel Christmas in the air," she shouted.

"Hooray!" said Baby Bear.

"I can feel it, too," said Harry Bear. "But I can also feel that my toes are still cold."

Four

Samantha Bear got a paper and pencil. She wrote Santa
a letter.

Dear Santa,

Do you remember your old friend Grandpa
Bear? He is the one who saved you from the
snowman. His coat is too small, and I am
worried he might catch a cold. Do you think
you could bring him a new coat?

Love,
Samantha Bear

P.S. You are invited to my Christmas play.

Mama Bear gave Samantha a stamp, and she took the letter to the mailbox. Then she went home to practice for the play.

"What are you going to be?" asked Harry Bear.

"I am going to be a toy in Santa's workshop," said Samantha. "I am going to be a mama doll."

"You are lucky," said Harry Bear. "In my Christmas play, I had to be a tree."

Samantha practiced very hard. She said "mama" very loudly. She said "mama" very softly. She said it in a high squeaky voice, and she said it in a low grumbly voice. She moved her arms like a doll.

At last it was Christmas Eve and time for the play.

"Oh, dear," said the teacher. "Mr. Grizzly is sick. Now what shall we do? The Santa Claus costume is too big for anyone else."

Samantha thought about Grandpa Bear's nice warm lap. She thought about his coat that wouldn't button over his nice big tummy. "Grandpa Bear is big enough," she told the teacher.

"Can he say, 'Ho! Ho! Ho!'?" asked the teacher.

"Oh, yes," said Samantha. "Santa himself taught him."

Samantha ran and got Grandpa Bear from the audience. Grandpa Bear put on the Santa Claus suit. He looked just like Santa.

At last the play could begin. The elves did a dance, and the Christmas trees sang a song about snow. Samantha waved her arms like a mama doll. She said "mama" in just the right voice.

"Ho! Ho! Ho!" said Grandpa Bear. He sounded just right, too.

Everyone cheered. "Wonderful," said Mama Bear.
"Not bad," said Harry Bear.
"Hooray!" said Baby Bear.
Someone else was cheering and clapping. Someone
with a red suit and a nice white beard. "Ho! Ho! Ho!" said
the someone. Then the someone slipped out of the door.

They all hung up their stockings when they got home from the play.

"What shall we leave for Santa?" asked Mama Bear.

"Cookies," said Samantha Bear.

"Chocolate cake," said Harry Bear.

"Both," said Grandpa Bear.

"I am going to stay awake and see Santa," said Harry Bear.

"So am I," said Samantha.

"You are too little," said Harry Bear. "You will fall asleep."

Samantha Bear snuggled in her bed. She kept her eyes wide open. She listened for reindeer on the roof.

Harry Bear did not see Santa Claus that night. He was sound asleep. But Santa saw Harry.

Samantha Bear did not see Santa Claus put the presents under the tree. But Santa saw Samantha snuggled deep in her bed.

Grandpa Bear did not see his old friend Santa that night. He was sound asleep in his chair by the fire. But Santa saw Grandpa. He left him a new coat with shiny gold buttons.

Baby Bear did see Santa Claus that night. Santa gave him a drink and tucked him back in bed.

"Hooray!" said Baby Bear.

"Ho! Ho! Ho!" said Santa. Then he went back up the chimney and got in his sleigh.

"Merry Christmas," called Santa, as his sleigh flew away. "Merry Christmas to all."